Selected Poetry of Boris Pasternak

Boris Pasternak

Selected Poetry of Boris Pasternak

ISBN: 978-1-63637-996-8

CONTENTS

A Dream

I dreamt of autumn in the window's twilight,
And you, a tipsy jesters' throng amidst.
And like a falcon, having stooped to slaughter,
My heart returned to settle on your wrist.

But time went on, grew old and deaf. Like thawing
Soft ice old silk decayed on easy chairs.
A bloated sunset from the garden painted
The glass with bloody red September tears.

But time grew old and deaf. And you, the loud one,
Quite suddenly were still. This broke a spell.
The dreaming ceased at once, as though in answer
To an abruptly silenced bell.

And I awakened. Dismal as the autumn
The dawn was dark. A stronger wind arose
To chase the racing birchtrees on the skyline,
As from a running cart the streams of straws.

A Walts With a Tear in It

Ah, how I love it in these first few days,
Fresh from the forest and out of the snow,
Awkwardness obvious still in every bough,
When every silver thread lazily sways
And every cone begins slowly to glow
In candlelight—and the white sheet below
Hides its sore stump from our eyes.

It will not bat an eye if you heap gold
And jewels on it-this shyest of fays
In blue enamel and tinfoil enfolded
Creeps in your heart of hearts—and there it stays.
Ah, how I love it all in these first days,
All golden finery and silver shades!

All in the making-stars, flags, lanterns, flares,
There are no chocolates yet in bonbonnieres.
Even the candles are no candles—they
Look more like dull sticks of makeup by day.
This is an actress still lighting stage fright
In the tumult of her benefit night.
Ah, how I love her on this opening day,
Flushed in the coulisses before the play!

Apples to appletrees, and kicks to firtrees.
Only not this one—no kicks for the beauty.
She has a different purpose and duty.
She's the select one, receiver of favours.
Her evening party will go on forever.
Others may fear proverb s-this one does not.

Her fate is only a few firtrees' lot.
Golden and fiery, she will soar high,
Like an old prophet ascending the sky.

Ah, how I love it all in these first days,
When all the world chats and fusses and plays!

After The Storm

The air is full of after-thunder freshness,
And everything rejoices and revives.
With the whole outburst of its purple clusters
The lilac drinks the air of paradise.

The gutters overflow; the change of weather
Makes all you see appear alive and new.
Meanwhile the shades of sky are growing lighter,
Beyond the blackest cloud the height is blue.

An artist's hand, with mastery still greater
Wipes dirt and dust off objects in his path.
Reality and life, the past and present,
Emerge transformed out of his colour-bath.

The memory of over half a lifetime
Like swiftly passing thunder dies away.
The century is no more under wardship:
High time to let the future have its say.

It is not revolutions and upheavals
That clear the road to new and better days,
But revelations, lavishness and torments
Of someone's soul, inspired and ablaze.

Autumn Frost

The morning sun shows like a pillar
Of fire through smoke on frosty days.
As on a faulty snap, it cannot
Make out my features in the haze.

The distant trees will hardly see me
Until the sun at last can break
Out of the fog, and flash triumphant
Upon the meadows by the lake.

A passer-by in mist receding
Is recognized when he has passed.
You walk on hoarfrost-covered pathways
As though on mats of plaited bast.

The frost is covered up in gooseflesh,
The air is false like painted cheeks,
The earth is shivering, and sick of
Breathing potato-stalks for weeks.

Black spring! Pick up your pen, and weeping...

Black spring! Pick up your pen, and weeping,
Of February, in sobs and ink,
Write poems, while the slush in thunder
Is burning in the black of spring.

Through clanking wheels, through church bells ringing
A hired cab will take you where
The town has ended, where the showers
Are louder still than ink and tears.

Where rooks, like charred pears, from the branches
In thousands break away, and sweep
Into the melting snow, instilling
Dry sadness into eyes that weep.

Beneath - the earth is black in puddles,
The wind with croaking screeches throbs,
And-the more randomly, the surer
Poems are forming out of sobs.

Craft

When, having finished, I shall move my armchair,
The page will gasp, awakened from the strain.
Delirious, she is half asleep at present,
Obedient to suspense and to the rain.

The heaviness of burnt-out ships has numbed her,
Prostrated, weighted down her senseless form;
You cannot dupe this one by false pretences-
It is the poet who will keep her warm.

I told her at an hour (its secret shudder
Vouchsafed by fancy) when the winter will
Light up green screeching ice, fed up with waiting
Behind an office worker's window sill,

And clocks in banks and other public places,
While drinking in the snow and outside's dark,
Will suddenly jump up and strike-their faces
Crossed by the clockhands at the "seven" mark-

At such a deep, at such a fateful hour,
I made the page wake up and take her chance,
To put on hood and scarf, and venture out to
Descendants, strangers, shaking off her trance.

Do not fret, do not cry, do not tax...

Do not fret, do not cry, do not tax
Your last strength, and your heart do not torture.
You're alive, you're inside me, intact,
As a buttress, a friend, an adventure.

I've no fear of standing exposed
As a fraud in my faith in the future.
It's not life, not a union of souls
We are breaking off, but a hoax mutual.

From straw mattresses' sick wretchedness
To the fresh air of wide open spaces!
It's my brother and hand. It's addressed
Like a letter, to you, crisp and bracing.

Like an envelope, tear it across,
With Horizon begin correspondence,
Give your speech the sheer Alpian force,
Overcome the sick sense of forlornness.

O'er the bowl of Bavarian lakes
With the marrow of osseous mountains
You will know I was not a glib fake
And of sugared assurances spouter.

Fare ye well and God bless you! Our bond
And our honour aren't tamely domestic.
Like a sprout in the sunlight, unbend,
And then things will assume a new aspect.

False Alarm

From early morning-nonsense
With tubs and troughs and strain,
With dampness in the evening
And sunsets in the rain.

Deep sighing of the darkness
And choking swallowed tears,
A railway engine's calling
Down from the sixteenth verst.

Outside and in the garden
A short fast-darkening day;
Small breakages and losses
In true September way.

In daytime autumn's vastness
Beyond the stream is rent
By wailing in the graveyard,
By anguish and lament.

But when the widow's sobbing
Is carried from the bank,
With all my blood I'm with her
And see my death point-blank.

As every year I see it
Out of the hall downstairs,
The long-delayed approaching
Of this my final year.

Through leaves in yellow terror,
Its way swept clear, I see
That winter from the hillside
Is staring down at me.

First Snow

Outside the snowstorm spins, and hides
   The world beneath a pall.
Snowed under are the paper-girl,
   The papers and the stall.

Quite often our experience
   Has led us to believe
That snow falls out of reticence,
   In order to deceive.

Concealing unrepentantly
   And trimming you in white,
How often he has brought you home
   Into the town at night!

While snowflakes blind and blanket out
   The distance more and more,
A tipsy shadow gropes his way
   And staggers to the door.

And then he enters hastily...
   Again, for all I know,
Someone has something sinful to
   Conceal in all this snow!

God's World

Thin as hair are the shadows of sunset
When they follow drawn-out every tree.
On the road through the forest the post-girl
Hands a parcel and letters to me.

By the trail of the cats and the foxes,
By the foxes' and by the cats' trail,
I return with a bundle of letters
To the house where my joy will prevail.

Countries, continents, isthmuses, frontiers,
Lakes and mountains, discussions and news,
Children, grown-ups, old folk, adolescents,
Appreciations, reports and reviews.

o respected and masculine letters!
All of you, none excepted, have brought
A display of intelligent logic
Underneath a dry statement of thought.

Precious, treasured epistles of women!
Why, I also fell down from a cloud.
And eternally now and for ever
To be yours I have solemnly vowed.

Well and you, stamp-collectors, if even
Only one fleeting moment you had
Among us, what a marvellous present
You would find in my sorrowful stead!

Here will be echoes in the mountains...

Here will be echoes in the mountains,
The distant landslides' rumbling boom,
The rocks, the dwellings in the village,
The sorry little inn, the gloom

Of something black beyond the Terek,
Clouds moving heavily. Up there
The day was breaking very slowly;
It dawned, but light was nowhere near.

One sensed the heaviness of darkness
For miles ahead around Kazbek
Wound on the heights: though some were trying
To throw the halter from their neck.

As if cemented in an oven,
In the strange substance of a dream,
A pot of poisoned food, the region
Of Daghestan there slowly steamed.

Its towering peaks towards us rolling,
All black from top to foot, it strained
To meet our car, if not with clashing
Of daggers, then with pouring rain.

The mountains were preparing trouble.
The handsome giants, fierce and black,
Each one more evil than the other
Were closing down upon our track.

How few are we. Probably three...

How few are we. Probably three
In all-coallike, burning, infernal
Beneath the grey bark of the tree
Of wisdom, and clouds, and eternal
Debate on verse, transport, the part
The army will play-and on art.

We used to be human. We're eras,
We're trains, in a caravan ripping
Through woods, to the sighing and fears
Of engines, and groans of the sleepers.
We'll rush in, and circle in the throes
Of being, like a whirlwind of crows.

A miss! Much too late you will see it.
Thus galloping wind in the morning
In passing a straw pile will buffet-
The blow will live on as a warning
To riotous tree-tops, and mingle
With their wrangles over the shingles.

I hang limp on the Creator's pen

I hang limp on the Creator's pen
Like a large drop of lilac gloss-paint.

Underneath are dykes' secrets; the air
From the railways is sodden and sticky,
Of the fumes of coal and night fires reeking.
But the moment night kills sunset's glare,
It turns pink itself, tinged with far flares,
And the fence stands stiff, paradox-stricken.

It keeps muttering: stop it till dawn.
Let the dry whiting finally settle.
Hard as nails is the worm-eaten ground,
And the echo's as keen as a skittle.

Warm spring wind, spots of cheviot and mud,
Early naileries' hoots faraway,
On the grater of cobble-stones road,
As on radishes lavishly sprayed,
Tears stand out clearly at break of day.

Like an acrid drop of thick lead paint,
I hang on to the Creator's pen.

Improvisation

I fed out of my hand a flock of keys
To clapping of wings and shrill cries in flight.
Sleeves up, arms out, on tiptoe I rose;
At my elbow I felt the nudging of night.
The dark. And the pond, and the wash of waves.
And screeching black beaks in their savage attack,
All quick for the kill - not to hunger and die,
While birds of the species I-love-you fall back.

The pond. And the dark. The pulsating flare
From pipkins of pitch in the gloom of midnight,
The boat keel nibbled by lapping of waves.
And birds at my elbow in their wrath and fight.
Night gurgled, washed in the gullets of weirs.
And it seemed if the young were unfed, by rote,
The hen-birds would kill - before the roulades
Would die in the shrilling, the crooked throat.

14

In Memory of Marina Tsvetaeva

Dismal day, with the weather inclement.
Inconsolably rivulets run
Down the porch in front of the doorway;
Through my wide-open windows they come.

But behind the old fence on the roadside,
See, the public gardens are flooded.
Like wild beasts in a den, the rainclouds
Sprawl about in shaggy disorder.

In such weather, I dream of a volume
On the beauties of Earth in our age,
And I draw an imp of the forest
Just for you on the title-page.

Oh, Marina, I'd find it no burden,
And the time has been long overdue:
Your sad clay should be brought from Yelabuga
By a requiem written for you.

All the triumph of your homecoming
I considered last year in a place
Near a snow-covered bend in the river
Where boats winter, locked in the ice.

What can I do to be of service?
Convey somehow your own request,
For in the silence of your going
There's a reproach left unexpressed.

A loss is always enigmatic.
I hunt for clues to no avail,
And rack my brains in fruitless torment:
Death has no lineaments at all.

Words left half-spoken, self-deception,
Promises, shadows-all are vain,
And only faith in resurrection
Can give the semblance of a sign.

Step out into the open country:
Winter's a sumptuous funeral wake.
Add currants to the dusk, then wine,
And there you have your funeral cake.

The apple-tree stands in a snowdrift
Outside. All this year long, to me,
The snow-clad city's been a massive
Monument to your memory.

With your face turned to meet your Maker.
You yearn for Him from here on Earth,
As in the days when those upon it
Were yet to appreciate your worth.

16

It's spring, I leave a street where poplars...

It's spring, I leave a street where poplars are astonished,
Where distance is alarmed and the house fears it may fall.
Where air is blue just like the linen bundle
A discharged patient takes from hospital,

Where dusk is empty, like a broken tale,
Abandoned by a star, without conclusion,
So that expressionless, unfathomable,
A thousand clamouring eyes are in confusion.

Marburg

I quivered. I flared up, and then was extinguished.
I shook. I had made a proposal - but late,
Too late. I was scared, and she had refused me.
I pity her tears, am more blessed than a saint.

I stepped into the square. I could be counted
Among the twice-born. Every leaf on the lime,
Every brick was alive, caring nothing for me,
And reared up to take leave for the last time.

The paving-stones glowed and the street's brow was swarthy,
From under their lids the cobbles looked grim,
Scowled up at the sky, and the wind like a boatman
Was rowing through limes. And each was an emblem.

Be that as it may, I avoided their glances,
Averted my gaze from their greeting or scowling.
I wanted no news of their getting and spending.
I had to get out, so as not to start howling.

The tiles were afloat, and an unblinking noon
Regarded the rooftops. And someone, somewhere
In Marburg, was whistling, at work on a crossbow,
And someone else dressing for the Trinity fair.

Devouring the clouds, the sand showed yellow,
A storm wind was rocking the bushes to and fro,
And the sky had congealed where it touched a sprig
Of woundwort that staunched its flow.

Like any rep Romeo hugging his tragedy,
I reeled through the city rehearsing you.
I carried you all that day, knew you by heart
From the comb in your hair to the foot in your shoe.

And when in your room I fell to my knees,
Embracing this mist, this perfection of frost
(How lovely you are!), this smothering turbulence,
What were you thinking? 'Be sensible!' Lost!

18

Here lived Martin Luther. The Brothers Grimm, there.
And all things remember and reach out to them:
The sharp-taloned roofs. The gravestones. The trees.
And each is alive. And each is an emblem.

I shall not go tomorrow. Refusal -
More final than parting. We're quits. áll is clear.
And if I abandon the streetlamps, the banks -
Old pavingstones, what will become of me here?

The mist on all sides will unpack its bags,
In both windows will hang up a moon.
And melancholy will slide over the books
And settle with one on the ottoman.

Then why am I scared? Insomnia I know
Like grammar, by heart. I have grown used to that.
In line with the four square panes of my window
Dawn will lay out her diaphanous mat.

The nights now sit down to play chess with me
Where ivory moonlight chequers the floor.
It smells of acacia, the windows are open,
And passion, a grey witness, stands by the door.

The poplar is king. I play with insomnia.
The queen is a nightingale I can hear calling.
I reach for the nightingale. And the night wins.
The pieces make way for the white face of morning.

Mary Magdalene I

As soon as night descends, we meet.
Remorse my memories releases.
The demons of the past compete,
And draw and tear my heart to pieces,
Sin, vice and madness and deceit,
When I was slave of men's caprices
And when my dwelling was the street.

The deathly silence is not far;
A few more moments only matter,
Which the Inevitable bar.
But at the edge, before they scatter,
In front of Thee my life I shatter,
As though an alabaster jar.

O what might not have been my fate
By now, my Teacher and my Saviour,
Did not eternity await
Me at the table, as a late
New victim of my past behaviour!

But what can sin now mean to me,
And death, and hell, and sulphur burning,
When, like a graft onto a tree,
I have-for everyone to see-
Grown into being part of Thee
In my immeasurable yearning?

When pressed against my knees I place
Thy precious feet, and weep, despairing,
Perhaps I'm learning to embrace
The cross's rough four-sided face;
And, fainting, all my being sways
Towards Thee, Thy burial preparing.

Music

The block of flats loomed towerlike.
Two sweating athletes, human telpher,
Were carrying up narrow stairs,
As though a bell onto a belfry,

As to a stony tableland
The tables of the law, with caution,
A huge and heavy concert-grand,
Above the city's restless ocean.

At last it stands on solid ground,
While deep below the din and clatter
Are damped, as though the town were drowned-
Sunk to the bottom of a legend.

The tenant of the topmost flat
Looks down on earth over the railings,
As if he held it in his hand,
Its lawful ruler, never failing.

Back in the drawing room he starts
To play-not someone else's music,
But his own thought, a new chorale,
The stir of leaves, Hosannas booming.

Improvisations sweep and peal,
Bring night, flames, fire barrels rolling,
Trees under downpour, rumbling wheels,
Life of the streets, fate of the lonely...

Thus Chopin would, at night, instead
Of the outgrown, naive and artless,
Write down on the black fretwork stand
His soaring dream, his new departures.

Or, overtaking in their flight
The world by many generations,
Valkyries shake the city roofs
By thunderous reverberations.

Or through the lovers' tragic fate,
Amidst infernal crash and thunder,
Tchaikovsky harrowed us to tears,
And rent the concert hall asunder.

Nostalgia

To give this book a dedication
The desert sickened,
And lions roared, and dawns of tigers
Took hold of Kipling.

A dried-up well of dreadful longing
Was gaping, yawning.
They swayed and shivered, rubbing shoulders,
Sleek-skinned and tawny.

Since then continuing forever
Their sway in scansion,
They stroll in mist through dewy meadows
Dreamt up by Ganges.

Creeping at dawn in pits and hollows
Cold sunrays fumble.
Funereal, incense-laden dampness
Pervades the jungle.

23

On a fateful day, an unlucky time

On a fateful day, an unlucky time,
Unannounced, it may happen thus:
Stifling, blacker still than a monastery
Utter madness descends on us.

Bitter frost. The night, as a decency,
Is observing the icy cold.
In an armchair, the ghost mumbles on and on,
Still the same, in his winter coat.

And the branch outside, and the parquet floor,
And his cheek, and the poker's shade-
All are shot with repentance and sleepiness
Of the blizzard that raved night and day.

Now the night is calm. Bright and frosty night.
Like a puppy suckling, still blind,
With the whole of their darkness-the palisade
Drinks the sparkle of stars through the pines.

Seems-it drips from them. Seems they're glimmering.
Seems-the night is brimming with wax
And the pad of one fir warms another pad
And one hollow traces the next.

Seems-this stillness, this height's an elegiac wave,
A concern of a soul for a mind,
The expectancy after an anxious "respond"!
Or an echo of different kind.

Seems it's dumb, this enquiring of needles and trees.
And the height is too deaf or too blue,
And the shine on the frozen swerve of the road's
A reply to that pleading "Helloooo..."

Bitter frost. The night, as a decency,
Is observing the icy cold.
In his armchair the ghost mumbles endlessly,
Still the same, in his winter coat-

24

Oh-his lips-he is squeezing them horribly!
Face in hands-shaking-ready to choke!
Whirls of clues for the gifted biographer
In this pattern, as dead as chalk.

Out of Superstition

A box of glazed sour fruit compact,
My narrow room.
And oh the grime of lodging rooms
This side the tomb!

This cubbyhole, out of superstition,
I chose once more.
The walls seem dappled oaks; the door,
A singing door.

You strove to leave; my hand was steady
Upon the latch.
My forelock touched a wondrous forehead;
My lips felt violets.

O Sweet! Your dress as on a day
Not long ago
To April, like a snowdrop, chirps
A gay "Hello!"

No vestal-you, I know: You came
With a chair today,
Took down my life as from a shelf,
And blew the dust away.

Poetry

Yes, I shall swear by you, my verse,
I shall wheeze out, before I swoon:
You're not a tenor's shape and voice,
You're summer travelling third class,
You are a suburb, not a tune.

You're a street as close as May,
You're a battlefield at night,
Where clouds groan loudly in dismay
And scatter, when dismissed, in fright.

And, splitting in the railway's lace-
That's outskirts, not refrain and home-
They crawl back to their native place
Without a song, as if struck dumb.

The shower's offshoots stick in clusters
Till break of day, and all the time
They scribble on the roofs acrostics
And bubble up rhyme after rhyme.

All poetry is what you make it.
And even when the truism's not worth
The rhyme, the flow of verse is scared.
The notebook's open-so flow forth!

Sometime at a concert hall, in recollection...

Sometime at a concert hall, in recollection,
A Brahms intermezzo will wound me-I'll start,
Remember that summer, the flowerbed garden,
The walks and the bathing, the tryst of six hearts,

The awkward, shy artist, with steep, dreamlike forehead,
Her smile, into which one would dive for a while,
A smile, as good-natured and bright as a river,
Her artist's appearance, her forehead, her smile.

They'll play me some Brahms-I will shudder, surrender,
And in retrospection the sounds will evoke
That faraway summer, the hoard of provisions,
My son and my brother, the garden, the oak.

The artist would stuff in her overall pockets
Her pencils, and objects with fanciful names,
Or would, inadvertently dropping her palette,
Turn much of the grass into colourful stains.

They'll play me some Brahms-I'll surrender, remember
The stubborn dry brushwood, the entrance, the roof,
Her smile and appearance, the mouth and the eyebrows,
The darkened verandah, the steps and the rooms.

And suddenly, as in a fairytale sequence,
The family, neighbours and friends will appear,
And-memories crowding-I'll drown in my weeping
Before I have time to have shed all my tears.

And, circling around in a swift intermezzo-
Embracing the song like a treetrunk at noon,
Four families' shadows will turn on the meadow
To Brahms's compelling and childhood-clear tune

Spring

This spring the world is new and different;
More lively is the sparrows' riot.
I do not even try expressing it,
How full my soul is and how quiet.

I think and write not as I did before;
And with their song of earth, entire
Freed territories add their mighty voice,
A booming octave in a choir.

The breath of spring within our motherland
Is washing off the winter's traces,
Is washing off black rings and crevices
From tear-worn eyes of Slavic races.

The grass is everywhere in readiness;
And ancient Prague, in murk and smother
Still silent, soon will be awakening,
One street more crooked than the other.

Morave and Czech and Jugoslavian
Folk-lores in spring will rise and blossom,
Tearing away the sheet of lawlessness
That winters past have laid across them.

It all will have the haze of fairy tales
Upon it, like the gilt and dazzle
Of ornaments in Boyar chambers and
On the cathedral of St Basil.

A dreamer and a half-night-ponderer,
Moscow I love with all my power.
Here is the source of all the wonderful
With which the centuries will flower.

Stars were racing

Stars were racing; waves were washing headlands.
Salt went blind, and tears were slowly drying.
Darkened were the bedrooms; thoughts were racing,
And the Sphinx was listening to the desert.

Candles swam. It seemed that the Colossus'
Blood grew cold; upon his lips was spreading
The blue shadow smile of the Sahara.
With the turning tide the night was waning.

Sea-breeze from Morocco touched the water.
Simooms blew. In snowdrifts snored Archangel.
Candles swam; the rough draft of 'The Prophet'
Slowly dried, and dawn broke on the Ganges.

The Girl

By a cliff a golden cloud once lingered;
    On his breast it slept...

From the swing, from the garden, helter-skelter,
    A twig runs up to the glass.
Enormous, close, with a drop of emerald
    At the tip of the cluster cast.

The garden is clouded, lost in confusion,
    In staggering, teeming fuss.
The dear one, as big as the garden, a sister
    By nature-a second glass!

But then this twig is brought in a tumbler
    And put by the looking-glass;
Which wonders:-Who is it that blurs my vision,
    From the dull, from the prison-class?

The Patient's Sweater

A life of its own and a long one is led
By this penguin, with nothing to do with the breast-
The wingless pullover, the patient's old vest;
Now pass it some warmth, move the lamp to the bed.

It dreams of the skiing; in darkness it poured
From shaftbows, from harness, from bodies; it seemed
That Christmas itself also sweated and snored;
The walking, the riding-all squeaked and all steamed.

A homestead, and horror and bareness beside,
Cut-glass in the sideboards, and carpets and chests;
The house was inflamed; this attracted the fence;
The lights swam in pleurisy, seen from outside.

Consumed by the sky, bloated shrubs on the way
Were white as a scare and had ice in their looks.
The blaze from the kitchen laid down by the sleigh
On the snow the enormous hands of the cooks.

The spring-it had simply been you

The spring-it had simply been you,
And so, to a certain extent,
The summer; but autumn-this scandalous blue
Of wallpaper? Rubbish and felt?

They lead an old horse to the knacker's yard.
His wistful, short-breathing nostrils
Are listening: wet camomile and moss,
Or maybe a whiff of horsemeat.

Imbibe with your lips and the blaze of your eyes
The transparent days' tear-stained vagueness,
Like the drift of an empty bottle of scent,
Its nostalgic lingering fragrance.

To sleep, not to argue. Despairingly
To sleep. Not to open the window
Where last summer, in frenzy, July
Was burning and glowing like jasper,
And melting the glass, and was pairing

The same crimson dragonflies,
Which now, on their nuptial beds,
Are deader and more transparent
Than crumbled dry cigarettes.

How sleepy and chilly are windows
In the twilight hours of frost.
Dry vitriol oil. At the bottom,
A gnat, and expired wasps.

How draughty the north is. How ruffled
And sulky... O whirlwind, drive,
Feel, search all the crannies and hollows,
Find me my song alive!

The Wind (Four fragments on Blok)

1

The most influential of nitwits,
The sycophant toadies are used
To rule who should live and be lauded
And who should be dead and abused.

Thus no one, maybe, could be certain,
Is Pushkin a poet or not,
Without their elaborate theses
Explaining to us what is what.

But Blok is, thank Heaven, another,
A different matter for once.
He did not descend from Sinai
And did not accept us as sons.

Eternal and not manufactured,
Renowned not according to plan,
Outside schools and systems, he has not
Been foisted upon us by man.

Three Variants

1

When in front of you hangs the day with its
    Smallest detail-fine or crude-
The intensely hot cracking squirrel-sounds
    Do not cease in the resinous wood.

The high line of pine-trees stands asleep,
    Drinking in and storing strength,
And the wood is peeling and drip by drip
    Is shedding freckled sweat.

2

From miles of calm the garden sickens,
    The stupor of the angered glen
Is more alarming than an evil
    Wild storm, a frightful hurricane.

The garden's mouth is dry, and smells of
    Decay, of nettles, roofing, fear...
The cattle's bellowing is closing
    Its ranks. A thunderstorm is near.

3

On the bushes grow the tatters
Of disrupted clouds; the garden
Has its mouth full of damp nettles:
Such - the smell of storms and treasures.

Tired shrubs are sick of sighing.
Patches in the sky increase. The
Barefoot blueness has the gait of
Cautious herons in the marshes.

And they gleam, like lips that glisten,
When the hand forgets to wipe them:
Supple willow-switches, oak-leaves,
And the hoofprints by the horsepond.

35

To Boris Pilnyak

Ah, don't I know that, groping in the gloom,
Night would not find its way out of the dark?
Am I monster who the millions' doom
Would shrug away for a few hundreds' luck?

Am I not measured by the Five-Year Plan?
Its falls and rises, aren't they also mine?
What shall I do, though, with my heartbeat, and
With things whose sluggishness boggles the mind?

In highest councils, in those spheres where reign
The highest passions and the strongest will,
The poet's post has been set up in vain:
It's dangerous-unless it's left unfilled.

Unique Days

How I remember solstice days
Through many winters long completed!
Each unrepeatable, unique,
And each one countless times repeated.

Of all these days, these only days,
When one rejoiced in the impression
That time had stopped, there grew in years
An unforgettable succession.

Each one of them I can evoke.
The year is to midwinter moving,
The roofs are dripping, roads are soaked,
And on the ice the sun is brooding.

Then lovers hastily are drawn
To one another, vague and dreaming,
And in the heat, upon a tree
The sweating nesting-box is steaming.

And sleepy clock-hands laze away
The clockface wearily ascending.
Eternal, endless is the day,
And the embrace is never-ending.

When It Clears Up

The lake is like a giant saucer;
Beyond-a gathering of clouds;
Like stern and dazzling mountain-ranges
Their massif the horizon crowds.

And with the light that swiftly changes,
The landscape never stays the same.
One moment clad in sooty shadows,
The next-the woods are all aflame.

When, after days of rainy weather,
The heavy curtain is withdrawn,
How festive is the sky, burst open!
How full of triumph is the lawn!

The wind dies down, the distance lightens,
And sunshine spreads upon the grass;
The steaming foliage is translucent
Like figures in stained-window glass.

Thus from the church's narrow windows
In glimmering crowns, on spreading wings
Gaze into time in sleepless vigil
Saints, hermits, prophets, angels, kings.

The whole wide world is a cathedral;
I stand inside, the air is calm,
And from afar at times there reaches
My ear the echo of a psalm.

World, Nature, Universe's Essence,
With secret trembling, to the end,
I will thy long and moving service
In tears of happiness attend.

Winter Night

It snowed and snowed ,the whole world over,
Snow swept the world from end to end.
A candle burned on the table;
A candle burned.

As during summer midges swarm
To beat their wings against a flame
Out in the yard the snowflakes swarmed
To beat against the window pane

The blizzard sculptured on the glass
Designs of arrows and of whorls.
A candle burned on the table;
A candle burned.

Distorted shadows fell
Upon the lighted ceiling:
Shadows of crossed arms,of crossed legs-
Of crossed destiny.

Two tiny shoes fell to the floor
And thudded.
A candle on a nightstand shed wax tears
Upon a dress.

All things vanished within
The snowy murk-white,hoary.
A candle burned on the table;
A candle burned.

A corner draft fluttered the flame
And the white fever of temptation
Upswept its angel wings that cast
A cruciform shadow

It snowed hard throughout the month
Of February, and almost constantly
A candle burned on the table;
A candle burned.

You are disappointed? You thought...

You are disappointed? You thought that in peace we
Would part to the sound of a requiem, a swan-song?
You counted on grief, with your pupils dilated,
    Their invincibility trying in tears on?

At the mass from the vaults then the murals had crumbled,
    By the play on the lips of Sebastian shaken...
But tonight to my hatred all seems drawn-out dawdling,
    What a pity there is not a whip for my hatred!

In darkness, collecting its wits instantaneously,
It knew without thinking: it would plough it over-
That it's time; that a suicide would be superfluous;
That this too would have been of a tortoise-like slowness.

A Sultrier Dawn

All morning high up on the eaves
Above your window
A dove kept cooing.
Like shirtsleeves The boughs seemed frayed.
It drizzled. Clouds came low to raid
The dusty marketplace.
My anguish on a peddlar's tray
They rocked;
I was afraid.
I begged the clouds that they should stop.
It seemed that they could hear me.
Dawn was as grey as in the shrub
Grey prisoners' angry murmur.

I pleaded with them to bring near
The hour when I would hear
Tidbits of shattered songs
And your wash-basin's roar and splash
Like mountain torrents' headlong rush,
The heat of cheek and brow
On glass as hot as ice and on
The pier-glass table flow.
My plea could not be heard on high
Because the clouds
Talked much too loud
Behind their flag in powdered quiet
Wet like a heavy army coat,
Like threshed sheaves' dusty rub-a-dub
Or like a quarrel in the shrub.

I pleaded with them-
Don't torment me!
I can't sleep.
But-it was drizzling; dragging feet,
The clouds marched down the dusty street
Like recruits from the village in the morning.
They dragged themselves along
An hour or an age,
Like prisoners of war,
Or like the dying wheeze:

41

"Nurse please,
Some water."

About These Poems

On winter pavements I will pound
Them down with glistening glass and sun,
Will let the ceiling hear their sound,
Damp corners-read them, one by one.

The attic will repeat my themes
And bow to winter with my lines,
And send leapfrogging to the beams
Bad luck and oddities and signs.

Snow will not monthly sweep and fall
And cover up beginnings, ends.
One day I'll suddenly recall:
The sun exists! Will see new trends,

Will see-the world is not the same;
Then, Christmas jackdaw-like will blink
And with a frosty day explain
What we, my love and I, should think.

The window-halves I'll throw apart,
In muffler from the cold to hide,
And call to children in the yard,
'What century is it outside?'

Who trod a trail towards the door,
The hole blocked up with sleet and snow,
The while I smoked with Byron or
Was having drinks with Edgar Poe?

While known in Darial or hell
Or armoury, as friend, I dipped
Like Lermontov's deep thrill, as well
My life in vermouth as my lips.

43

August

This was its promise, held to faithfully:
The early morning sun came in this way
Until the angle of its saffron beam
Between the curtains and the sofa lay,

And with its ochre heat it spread across
The village houses, and the nearby wood,
Upon my bed and on my dampened pillow
And to the corner where the bookcase stood.

Then I recalled the reason why my pillow
Had been so dampened by those tears that fell-
I'd dreamt I saw you coming one by one
Across the wood to wish me your farewell.

You came in ones and twos, a straggling crowd;
Then suddenly someone mentioned a word:
It was the sixth of August, by Old Style,
And the Transfiguration of Our Lord.

For from Mount Tabor usually this day
There comes a light without a flame to shine,
And autumn draws all eyes upon itself
As clear and unmistaken as a sign.

But you came forward through the tiny, stripped,
The pauperly and trembling alder grove,
Into the graveyard's coppice, russet-red,
Which, like stamped gingerbread, lay there and glowed.

And with the silence of those high treetops
Was neighbour only the imposing sky
And in the echoed crowing of the cocks
The distances and distances rang by:

There in the churchyard underneath the trees,
Like some surveyor from the government
Death gazed on my pale face to estimate
How large a grave would suit my measurement.

All those who stood there could distinctly hear
A quiet voice emerge from where I lay:
The voice was mine, my past; prophetic words
That sounded now, unsullied by decay:

'Farewell, wonder of azure and of gold
Surrounding the Transfiguration's power:
Assuage now with a woman's last caress
The bitterness of my predestined hour!

'Farewell timeless expanse of passing years!
Farewell, woman who flung your challenge steeled
Against the abyss of humiliations:
For it is I who am your battlefield!

'Farewell, you span of open wings outspread,
The voluntary obstinacy of flight,
O figure of the world revealed in speech,
Creative genius, wonder-working might!'

Bad Days

When Passion week started and Jesus
Came down to the city, that day
Hosannahs burst out at his entry
And palm leaves were strewn in his way.

But days grow more stern and more stormy.
No love can men's hardness unbend;
Their brows are contemptuously frowning,
And now comes the postscript, the end.

Grey, leaden and heavy, the heavens
Were pressing on treetops and roofs.
The Pharisees, fawning like foxes,
Were secretly searching for proofs.

The lords of the Temple let scoundrels
Pass judgement, and those who at first
Had fervently followed and hailed him,
Now all just as zealously cursed.

The crowd on the neighbouring sector
Was looking inside through the gate.
They jostled, intent on the outcome,
Bewildered and willing to wait.

And whispers and rumours were creeping,
Repeating the dominant theme.
The flight into Egypt, his childhood
Already seemed faint as a dream.

And Jesus remembered the desert,
The days in the wilderness spent,
The tempting with power by Satan,
That lofty, majestic descent.

He thought of the wedding at Cana,
The feast and the miracles; and
How once he had walked on the waters
Through mist to a boat, as on land;

The beggarly crowd in a hovel,
The cellar to which he was led;
How, started, the candle-flame guttered,
When Lazarus rose from the dead...

Change

I used to glorify the poor,
Not simply lofty views expressing:
Their lives alone, I felt, were true,
Devoid of pomp and window-dressing.

No stranger to the manor house,
Its finery and lordly tenor,
I was a friend of down-and-outs,
And shunned the idly sponging manner.

For choosing friendship in the ranks
Of working people, though no rebel,
I had the honour to be stamped
As also one among the rabble.

The state of basements, unadorned,
Of attics with no frills or curtains
Was tangible without pretence
And full of substance, weighty, certain.

And I went bad when rot defaced
Our time, and life became infested,
When grief was censured as disgrace
And all played optimists and yes-men.

My faith in those who seemed my friends
Was broken and our ties were sundered.
I, too, lost Man, the Human, since
He had been lost by all and sundry.

Definition of Creative Art

With shirt wide open at the collar,
Maned as Beethoven's bust, it stands;
Our conscience, dreams, the night and love,
Are as chessmen covered by its hands.

And one black king upon the board:
In sadness and in rage, forthright
It brings the day of doom.-Against
The pawn it brings the mounted knight.

In gardens where from icy spheres
The stars lean tender, linger near,
Tristan still sings, like a nightingale
On Isolde's vine, with trembling fear.

The gardens, ponds, and fences, made pure
By burning tears, and the whole great span,
Creation-are only burst of passion
Hoarded in the hearts of men.

Eve

Definition of Creative Art

By water's edge, quiet willows stand,
And from the steep bank, high noon flings
White fleecy clouds into the pond
    As if they were a fisher's seines.

The firmament sinks like a net,
A crowd of sunburnt bathers dive
With yells into the pond, and head
    For this elusive netlike sky.

Some women from the water rise
    Under the scanty willows' lee,
And stepping on the sand, wring dry
Their bathing costumes hurriedly.

The coils of fabric twist and slide
Like water-snakes, and nimbly roll,
As if the dripping garments hide
Beguiling serpents in their folds.

o woman, neither looks nor shape
Will nonplus me or make me gloat.
    You, all of you, are like a lump
In my excitement-stricken throat.

You look as if hewn in the rough-
A stray verse line dashed off ad lib.
You make me think it is the truth-
That you were made out of my rib.

And instantly you broke away
From my embrace, and moved apart,
    All fear, confusion, disarray-
And missing beats of a man's heart.

Feasts

I drink the gall of skies in autumn, tuberoses'
Sweet bitterness in your betrayals burning stream;
I drink the gall of nights, of crowded parties' noises,
Of sobbing virgin verse, and of a throbbing dream.

We fiends of studious fight a battle everlasting
Against our daily bread - can't stand the sober mood.
The troubled wind of nights is merely a toastmaster
Whose toasts, as like as not, will do no one much good.

Heredity and death are our guests at table.
A quiet dawn will paint bright-red the tops of trees.
An anapaest, like mice, will on the bread-plate scrabble,
And Cinderella will rush in to change her dress.

The floors have all been swept, and everything is dainty,
And like a child's sweet kiss, breathes quietly my verse,
And Cinderella flees-by cab on days of plenty,
And on shanks' pony when the last small coin is lost.

From A Poem

I also loved, and the restless breaths
Of sleeplessness, fluttering through darkness,
Out of the park would downward drift
To the ravine, on to the archipelago
Of meadows, sinking from sight among
Wormwood, mint and quails beneath the wispy mist.
And the broad sweep of adoration's wing grew
Heavy and drunken, as though stung by shot,
Floundered into the air and, shuddering, fell short,
Scattering across the fields as dew.

And then the dawn was breaking. Till two
Rich jewels blinked in the incalculable sky,
But then the cocks began to feel afraid
Of darkness and strove to hide their fright,
But in their throats blank mines exploded,
As they strained, fear's putrid voice erupted.
As though by order, as the constellations faded,
A shepherd, goggle-eyed as though from snuffing candles,
Made his appearance where the forest ended.

I also loved and she, it well may be,
Is living yet. The time will pass on by
Till something large as autumn, one fine day,
(If not tomorrow, then perhaps some other time)
Will blaze out over life like sunset's glow, in pity
For the thicket. For the foolish puddle's tormenting,
Toadish thirst. For the clearings trembling timidly
As hares, their ears tight-muffled in the wrapping
Of last year's fallen leaves. For the noise, as though
False waves are pounding on the shores of long ago.
I also loved, and know: as damp mown fields
Are laid by the ages at each year's feet,
So the fevering newness of the worlds is laid
By love at the bed-head of every heart.

I also loved, and she is living still.
Cascading into that first earliness, as ever
Time stands still, vanishing away as it spills
Over the moment's edge. Subtle as ever this boundary.

52

Still as before, how recent seems the long ago.
Time past streams from the faces of those who saw,
Playing still its crazy tricks, as if it did not know
It has no tenancy in our house any more.
Can it be so? Does love really not last,
This momentary tribute of bright wonderment,
But ever, all our life, recede into the past?

Hamlet

The murmurs ebb; onto the stage I enter.
I am trying, standing in the door,
To discover in the distant echoes
What the coming years may hold in store.

The nocturnal darkness with a thousand
Binoculars is focused onto me.
Take away this cup, O Abba Father,
Everything is possible to Thee.

I am fond of this Thy stubborn project,
And to play my part I am content.
But another drama is in progress,
And, this once, O let me be exempt.

But the plan of action is determined,
And the end irrevocably sealed.
I am alone; all round me drowns in falsehood:
Life is not a walk across a field.

Here—now—our age of socialism!...

Here—now—our age of socialism!
Here in the thick of life below.
Today in the name of things to be
Into the future forth we go.

Like Georgia shining in her beauty,
Like a land of light by open seas,
It beckons-veiled within a mist
Of wild surmise and theories.

There mothers of Putivl no more
Lament like cuckoos their dismay;
There joy no longer looks askance
In fear, but walks abroad by day.

There life and happiness converse
Together, free from hate and strife,
All joined to give their saving strength
And stay to every child and wife.

There men no longer by exchange
Compute the things they have or owe,
But gladly spend themselves in giving-
The all they have, the all they know.

Then let my message overtake
This wondrous age in history:
O may my children in their gladness
Out of the future answer me!

Humble home. But rum, and charcoal...

Humble home. But rum, and charcoal
Grog of sketches on the wall,
And the cell becomes a mansion,
And the garret is a hall.

No more waves of housecoats: questions,
Even footsteps disappear;
Glassy mica fills the latticed
Work-encompassed vault of air.

Voice, commanding as a levy,
Does not leave a thing immune,
Smelting, fusing... In his gullet
Flows the tin of molten spoons.

What is fame for him, and glory,
Name, position in the world,
When the sudden breath of fusion
Blends his words into the Word?

He will burn for it his chattels,
Friendship, reason, daily round.
On his desk-a glass, unfinished,
World forgotten, clock unwound.

Clustered stanzas change like seething
Wax at fortune-telling times.
He will bless the sleeping children
With the steam of molten rhymes.

I would go home again—to rooms...

I would go home again—to rooms
With sadness large at eventide,
Go in, take off my overcoat,
And in the light of streets outside

Take cheer. I'll pass the thin partitions
Right through; yes, like a beam I'll pass,
As image blends into an image,
As one mass splits another mass.

Let all abiding mooted problems
Deep rooted in our fortunes seem
To some a sedentary habit;
But still at home I brood and dream.

Again the trees and houses breathe
Their old refrain and fragrant air.
Again to right and left old winter
Sets up her household everywhere.

Again by dinner time the dark
Comes suddenly—to blind, to scare,
To teach the narrow lanes and alleys
She'll fool them if they don't take care.

Again, though weak my heart, O Moscow,
I listen, and in words compose
The way you smoke, the way you rise,
The way your great construction goes.

And so I take you as my harness
For the sake of raging days to be,
That you may know our past by heart
And like a poem remember me.

In everything I seek to grasp...

In everything I seek to grasp
The fundamental:
The daily choice, the daily task,
The sentimental.

To plumb the essence of the past,
The first foundations,
The crux, the roots, the inmost hearts,
The explanations.

And, puzzling out the weave of fate,
Events observer,
To live, feel, love and meditate
And to discover.

Oh, if my skill did but suffice
After a fashion,
In eight lines I'd anatomize
The parts of passion.

I'd write of sins, forbidden fruit,
Of chance-seized shadows;
Of hasty flight and hot pursuit,
Of palms, of elbows.

Define its laws and origin
In terms judicial,
Repeat the names it glories in,
And the initials.

I'd sinews strain my verse to shape
Like a trim garden:
The limes should blossom down the nape,
A double cordon.

My verse should breathe the fresh-clipped hedge,
Roses and meadows
And mint and new-mown hay and sedge,
The thunder's bellows.

As Chopin once in his etudes
Miraculously conjured
Parks, groves, graves and solitudes-
A living wonder.

The moment of achievement caught
Twixt sport and torment...
A singing bowstring shuddering taut,
A stubborn bow bent.

Intoxication

Under osiers with ivy ingrown
We are trying to hide from bad weather.
I am clasping your arms in my own,
In one cloak we are huddled together.

I was wrong. Not with ivy-leaves bound,
But with hops overgrown is the willow.
Well then, let us spread out on the ground
This our cloak as a sheet and a pillow.

July

A ghost is roaming through the building,
And shadows in the attic browse;
Persistently intent on mischief
A goblin roams about the house.

He gets into your way, he fusses,
You hear his footsteps overhead,
He tears the napkin off the table
And creeps in slippers to the bed.

With feet unwiped he rushes headlong
On gusts of draught into the hall
And whirls the curtain, like a dancer,
Towards the ceiling, up the wall.

Who is this silly mischief-maker,
This phantom and this double-face?
He is our guest, our summer lodger,
Who spends with us his holidays.

Our house is taken in possession
By him, while he enjoys a rest.
July, with summer air and thunder-
He is our temporary guest.

July, who scatters from his pockets
The fluff of blow-balls in a cloud,
Who enters through the open window,
Who chatters to himself aloud,

Unkempt, untidy, absent-minded,
Soaked through with smell of dill and rye,
With linden-blossom, grass and beet-leaves,
The meadow-scented month July.

March

The sun is hotter than the top ledge in a steam bath;
The ravine, crazed, is rampaging below.
Spring — that corn-fed, husky milkmaid —
Is busy at her chores with never a letup.

The snow is wasting (pernicious anemia —
See those branching veinlets of impotent blue?)
Yet in the cowbarn life is burbling, steaming,
And the tines of pitchforks simply glow with health.

These days — these days, and these nights also!
With eavesdrop thrumming its tattoos at noon,
With icicles (cachectic!) hanging on to gables,
And with the chattering of rills that never sleep!

All doors are flung open — in stable and in cowbarn;
Pigeons peck at oats fallen in the snow;
And the culprit of all this and its life-begetter—
The pile of manure — is pungent with ozone.

Mary Magdalene II

People clean their homes before the feast.
Stepping from the bustle of the street
I go down before Thee on my knees
And anoint with myrrh Thy holy feet.

Groping round, I cannot find the shoes
For the tears that well up with my sighs.
My impatient tresses, breaking loose,
Like a pall hang thick before my eyes.

I take up Thy feet onto my lap,
Wash them clean with hot tears from my eyes,
In my hair Thy precious feet I wrap,
And my string of pearls around them tie.

I now see the future in detail,
As if it were stopped in flight by Thee.
Like a raving sibyl, I could tell
What will happen, how it will all be.

In the temple, veils will fall tomorrow,
We shall form a frightened group apart,
And the earth will shake-perhaps from sorrow
And from pity for my tortured heart.

Troops will then reform and march away
To the thud of hoofs and heavy tread,
And the cross will reach towards the sky
Like a water-spout above our heads.

By the cross, I'll fall down on the ground,
I shall bite my lips till I draw blood.
On the cross, your arms will be spread out-
Wide enough to hug the whole wide world.

Who's this for, this glory and this strife?
Who's this for, this torment and this might?
Are there enough souls on earth, and lives?
Are there enough cities, dales and heights?

63

But three days-such days and nights will pass-
They will fill me with such crushing dread
That I'll see the joyous truth, at last:
I shall know Christ will rise from the dead.

My desk is not so wide that I might lean

My desk is not so wide that I might lean
Against the edge and reach out past the shell
Of board and glass, beyond the isthmus in
The endless miles of my scraped out farewell.

(It's night there now.) Beyond your sultry neck.
(They went to bed.) Behind your shoulders' realm.
(Switched off the light.) At dawn, I'd give them back.
The porch would touch them with a sleepy stem.

No, not with snowflakes! With your arms! Reach far!
Oh you, ten fingers of my pain, the light
Of crystal winter stars-and every star
A sign of northbound snowbound trains being late.

O had I known that thus it happens...

O had I known that thus it happens,
When first I started, that at will
Your lines with blood in them destroy you,
Roll up into your throat and kill,

My answer to this kind of joking
Had been a most decisive 'no'.
So distant was the start, so timid
The first approach-what could one know?

But older age is Rome, demanding
From actors not a gaudy blend
Of props and reading, but in earnest
A tragedy, with tragic end.

A slave is sent to the arena
When feeling has produced a line.
Tnen breathing soil and fate take over
And art has done and must resign.

On Early Trains

This winter I was outside Moscow,
But when the time for work came round,
Through the blizzard, biting frost and snow,
    I made the journey into town.

At the hour I stepped outside the door
Not a soul could be seen on the street,
And through the forest darkness drifted forth
    The crunching echo of my tramping feet.

At the crossing I was greeted
By the willows of the vacant plot.
The constellations towered above the world
    In the dark chill of January's pit.

And usually, there behind the yards,
The number forty or the early mail
Would overhaul me, pulling hard,
    But the six forty-five was my own train.

Suddenly some invisible tentacles
Would draw into a circle lines of light,
As a massive searchlight hurtled past
    On to the viaduct out of the night.

Once in the carriage's tuffy heat
I would allow myself to sink
Into the state of innate weakness
    I imbibed with my mother's milk.

Through all the struggles of the past,
Through all the years of war and want,
I gazed on Russia'a unique face
    In silent awe and wonderment.

Passing beyond this adoration,
I worshipped as I looked around
At countrywomen, students, workers
    Living on the edge of town.

I could not see a single trace
Of servitude imposed by poverty.
Each new discomfort and each change
Was borne with lordly dignity.

Bunched close together in a group,
Boys and girls sat reading there,
Struck varied poses as they read,
Drinking in the words like vital air.

Moscow greeted us in darkness
Already lined with silver light,
As we emerged from underground,
Out of the ambiguity of night.

Our future pressed against the rails,
Flooding my senses as they went,
With floral soap's lingering trace
And honey-cakes' enticing scent.

Parting

A man is standing in the hall
His house not recognizing.
Her sudden leaving was a flight,
Herself, maybe, surprising.

The chaos reigning in the room
He does not try to master.
His tears and headache hide in gloom
The extent of his disaster.

His ears are ringing all day long
As though he has been drinking.
And why is it that all the time
Of waves he keeps on thinking?

When frosty window-panes blank out
The world of light and motion,
Despair and grief are doubly like
The desert of the ocean.

She was as dear to him, as close
In all her ways and features,
As is the seashore to the wave,
The ocean to the beaches.

As over rushes, after storm
The swell of water surges,
Into the deepness of his soul
Her memory submerges.

In years of strife, in times which were
Unthinkable to live in,
Upon a wave of destiny
To him she had been driven,

Through countless obstacles, and past
All dangers never-ended,
The wave had carried, carried her,
Till close to him she'd landed.

69

And now, so suddenly, she'd left.
What power overrode them?
The parting will destroy them both,
The grief bone-deep corrode them.

He looks around him. On the floor
In frantic haste she'd scattered
The contents of the cupboard, scraps
Of stuff, her sewing patterns.

He wanders through deserted rooms
And tidies up for hours;
Till darkness falls he folds away
Her things into the drawers;

And pricks his finger on a pin
In her unfinished sewing,
And sees the whole of her again,
And silent tears come flowing.

Railway Station

My dear railway station, my treasure
Of meetings and partings, my friend
In times of hard trials and pleasure,
Your favours have been without end.

My scarf would wrap up my whole being -
The train would pull up, with deep sighs,
The muzzles of brash harpies, leering,
Would puff wet white steam in our eyes.

I'd sit at your side for a moment -
A hug and a kiss, brief and rough.
Farewell then, my joy and my torment.
I'm going, conductor, I'm off!

And, shunting bad weather and sleepers,
The west would break open-I'd feel
It grab me with snowflakes to keep me
From falling down under the wheels.

A whistle dies down, echoed weakly,
Another flies from distant tracks.
A train comes past bare platforms sweeping -
A blizzard of many hunched backs.

And twilight is rearing to go,
And, lured by the smoke and the steam,
The wind and the field rush and now
I wish I could be one of them!

Soul

My mournful soul, you, sorrowing
    For all my friends around,
You have become the burial vault
    Of all those hounded down.

Devoting to their memory
    A verse, embalming them,
In torment, broken, lovingly
    Lamenting over them,

In this our mean and selfish time,
    For conscience and for quest
You stand-a columbarium
    To lay their souls to rest.

The sum of all their agonies
    Has bowed you to the ground.
You smell of dust, of death's decay,
    Of morgue and burial mound.

My beggarly, dejected soul,
    You heard and saw your fill;
Remembered all and mixed it well,
    And ground it like a mill.

Continue pounding and compound
    All that I witnessed here
To graveyard compost, as you did
    For almost forty years.

Spring (Fragment 3)

Is it only dirt you notice?
Does the thaw not catch your glance?
As a dapple-grey fine stallion
Does it not through ditches dance?

Is it only birds that chatter
In the blueness of the skies,
Sipping through the straws of sunrays
Lemon liturgies on ice?

Only look, and you will see it:
From the rooftops to the ground
Moscow, all day long, like Kitezh
Lies, in light-blue water drowned.

Why are all the roofs transparent
And the colours crystal-bright?
Bricks like rushes gently swaying,
Mornings rush into the night.

Like a bog the town is swampy
And the scabs of snow are rare.
February, like saturated
Cottonwool in spirits, flares.

This white flame wears out the garrets,
And the air, in the oblique
Interplace of twigs and birds, is
Naked, weightless and unique.

In such days the crowds of people
Knock you down; you are unknown,
Nameless; and your girl is with them,
But you, too, are not alone.

Sultry Night

It drizzled, but not even grasses
Would bend within the bag of storm;
Dust only gulped its rain in pellets,
The iron roof-in powder form.

The village did not hope for healing.
Deep as a swoon the poppies yearned
Among the rye in inflammation,
And God in fever tossed and turned.

In all the sleepless, universal,
The damp and orphaned latitude,
The sighs and moans, their posts deserting,
Fled with the whirlwind in pursuit.

Behind them ran blind slanting raindrops
Hard on their heels, and by the fence
The wind and dripping branches argued-
My heart stood still-at my expense.

I felt this dreadful garden chatter
Would last forever, since the street
Would also notice me, and mutter
With bushes, rain and window shutter.

No way to challenge my defeat-
They'd argue, talk me off my feet.

The Linden Avenue

A house of unimagined beauty
Is set in parkland, cool and dark;
Gates with an arch; then meadows, hillocks,
And oats and woods beyond the park.

Here, with their crowns each other hiding,
Enormous linden trees engage
In dusky, quiet celebration
Of their two hundred years of age.

And underneath their vaulted branches,
Across the regularly drawn
Symmetric avenues, grow flowers
In flower-beds upon a lawn.

Beneath the trees, on sandy pathways,
Not one bright spot relieves the dark,
Save-like an opening in a tunnel-
The distant entrance of the park.

But now the blossom-time is starting,
The walled-in linden trees reveal
And spread about within their shadow
Their irresistible appeal.

The visitors, in summer clothing,
While walking on the crunchy sand,
Breathe in unfathomable fragrance
Which only bees can understand.

This gripping scent is theme and subject,
Whereas-however well they look-
The flower-beds, the lawn, the garden,
Are but the cover of a book.

The clustered, wax-bespattered flowers
On massive trees, sedate and old,
Lit up by raindrops, burn and sparkle
Above the mansion they enfold.

The Road

Down into the ravine, then forward
Up the embankment to the top,
The ribbon of the road runs snaking
Through wood and field without a stop.

By all the precepts of perspective
Well-surfaced highway windings rush
Among the fields, among the meadows,
Not raising dust, nor stuck in slush.

The peaceful pond nearby ignoring
(On which a duck with ducklings swam)
The road once more is forward soaring
On having crossed and left the dam.

Now-down a slope again it hastens,
Now-on and upwards, in a climb,
As only life, maybe, is meant to
Strain up and onward all the time.

Through thousands of unheard-of fancies,
Through times and countries, climb and fall,
Through helps and hindrances it races
Relentless, too, towards a goal;

And this is to have lived your fullest,
Experienced all-at home, abroad-
Just as the landscape now is livened
By twists and turnings of the road.

The Swifts

The swifts have no strength any more to retain,
To check the light-blue evening coolness.
It burst from their breasts, from their throats, under strain
And flows out of hand in its fullness.

There is not a thing that could stop them, up there,
From shrilly, exultedly crying,
Exclaiming: The earth has made off to nowhere,
O look! It has vanished - O triumph!

As cauldrons of water are ended in steam
When quarrelsome bubbles are rising -
Look - there is no room for the earth - from the seam
Of the gorge to the drawn-out horizon!

There'll be no one in the house...

There'll be no one in the house
Save for twilight. All alone,
Winter's day seen in the space that's
Made by curtains left undrawn.

Only flash-past of the wet white
Snowflake clusters, glimpsed and gone.
Only roofs and snow, and save for
Roofs and snow-no one at home.

Once more, frost will trace its patterns,
I'll be haunted once again
By my last year's melancholy,
By that other wintertime.

Once more, I'll be troubled by an
Old unexpiated shame,
And the icy firewood famine
Will press on the window-pane.

But the quiver of intrusion
Through those curtains folds will run.
Measuring silence with your footsteps,
Like the future, in you'll come.

You'll appear there in the doorway
Wearing something white and plain,
Something in the very stuff from
Which the snowflakes too are sewn.

Thunderstorm, Instantaneous Forever

After this the halt and summer
Parted company; and taking
Off his cap at night the thunder
Took a hundred blinding stills.

Lilac clusters faded; plucking
Off an armful of new lightnings,
From the field he tried to throw them
At the mansion in the hills.

And when waves of evil laughter
Rolled along the iron roofing
And, like charcoal on a drawing,
Showers thundered on the fence,

Then the crumbling mind began to
Blink; it seemed it would be floodlit
Even in those distant comers
Where the light is now intense.

To the Memory of Demon

Used to come in the blue
Of the glacier, at night, from Tamara.
With his wingtips he drew
Where the nightmares should boom, where to bar them.

Did not sob, nor entwine
The denuded, the wounded, the ailing...
A stone slab has survived
By the Georgian church, at the railings.

Hunchback shadows, distressed,
Did not dance by the fence of the temple.
Soft, about the princess
The zurna did not question the lamplight,

But the sparks in his hair
Were aglitter and bursting phosphorous,
And the giant did not hear
The dark Caucasus greying for sorrow.

Venice

A click of window glass had roused me
Out of my sleep at early dawn.
Beneath me Venice swam in water;
A sodden pretzel made of stone.

I was all quiet now; however,
While still asleep, I heard a cry -
And like a sign that had been silenced
It still disturbed the morning sky.

It hung - a trident of the Scorpion -
Above the sleeping mandolins
And had been uttered by an angry
Insulted woman's voice, maybe.

Now it was silent. To the handle
Its fork was stuck in morning haze.
The Grand Canal, obliquely grinning
Kept looking back - a runaway

. . . .

Reality was born of dream-shreds
Far off, among the hired boats.
Like a Venetian woman, Venice
Dived from the bank to glide afloat.

81

White Night

I keep thinking of times that are long past,
Of a house in the Petersburg Quarter.
You had come from the steppeland Kursk Province,
Of a none-too-rich mother the daughter.

You were nice, you had many admirers.
On that distant white night we were sitting
On your window-sill, looking from high on
On the phantom-like scene of the city.

The street-lamps, like gauze butterflies fluttering,
Had been touched by the chill of the morning.
My soft words, as I opened my heart to you,
Matched the slumbering vistas before us.

We were plighted with timid fidelity
To the very same nebulous mystery
As the cityscape spreading unendingly
Far beyond the Neva, through the distances.

In that far-off impregnable wilderness,
Wrapped in springtime twilight ethereal,
Woodland glades and dense thickets were quivering
With mad nightingales' thunderous paeans.

Crazy resonant warbling ran riot,
And the voice of this plain-looking songster
Sowed derangement, ecstatic delight
In the depth of the mesmerised copsewood.

To those parts Night, a barefoot vagabond,
Stole its way along ditches and fences.
From our window-sill, after it tagging,
Was the trail of our cooed confidences.

To the words of this colloquy echoing
In the orchards beyond the tall palings
Spreading branches of apple and cherry trees
Swathed themselves in their pearly-white raiment.

And the trees, like so many pale phantoms,
Waved their farewell, along the road thronging,
To White Night, that all-seeing enchanter,
Who was now to North Regions withdrawing.

With Oars at Rest

A boat is beating in the breast of the lake.
Willows hang over, tickling and kissing
Neckline and knuckles and rowlocks-O wait,
This could have happened to anyone, listen!

This could be used in a song, to beguile.
This then would mean-the ashes of lilac,
Richness of dew-drenched and crushed camomile,
Bartering lips for a start after twilight.

This is-embracing the firmament; strong
Hercules holding it, clasping still fonder.
This then would mean-whole centuries long
Fortunes for nightingales' singing to squander.

Your Picture

It's with your laughing picture that I'm living now,
You whose wrists are so slender and crackle at the joints,
You who wring your hands yet are unwilling to go,
You whose guests stay for hours sharing sadness and joys.

You who'll run from the cards and Rakoczy bravura,
From the glass of the drawing-room and from the guests
To the keyboard on fire, unable to endure
Bones and roses and dice and rosettes and the rest.

You will fluff up your hair, and a reckless tea-rose,
Smelling of cigarettes, pin to your bright-red sash,
And then waltz to your glory, your sadness and woes
Tossing off like a scarf, beaming, breathless and flushed.

You will crumple the skin of an orange and swallow
Cooling morsels again and again in your haste
To return to the hall, to the whirling and mellow
Lights, and air with the sweet sweat of fresh waltzes laced.

Defying steam and scorching breath
The way a whirlwind dies,
The way a murid faces death
With wide unflinching eyes.

Know all: not mountains' noise and hush,
And not a purebred steed-
The reckless roses in your sash
Are riding at full speed.

No, not the clatter of the hoofs
And not the mountains' hush,
But only she who stands aloof
With flowers in her sash.

And only that is really It
What makes our ears ring,
And what the whirlwind-chasing feet,
Soul, tulle and silk sash bring.

Until sides split the jokes are cracked,
We're rolling in the aisles,
The envy of the romping sacks-
Until somebody cries.

A tall, strapping shot, you, considerate hunter...

A tall, strapping shot, you, considerate hunter,
Phantom with gun at the flood of my soul,
Do not destroy me now as a traitor,
As fodder for feeling, crumbled up small!

Grant me destruction rising and soaring,
Dress me at night in the willow and ice.
Start me, I pray, from the reeds in the morning,
Finish me off with one shot in my flight,

And for this lofty and resonant parting
Thank you. Forgive me, I kiss you, oh hands
Of my neglected, my disregarded
Homeland, my diffidence, family, friends.

After the Interval

About three months ago, when first
Upon our open, unprotected
And freezing garden snowstorms burst
In sudden fury, I reflected

That I would shut myself away
And in seclusion write a section
Of winter poems, day by day,
To supplement my spring collection.

But nonsense piled up mountain-high,
Like snow-drifts hindering and stifling
And half the winter had gone by,
Against all hopes, in petty trifling.

I understood, alas, too late
Why winter-while the snow was falling,
Piercing the darkness with its flakes-
From outside at my house was calling;

And while with numb white-frozen lips
It whispered, urging me to hurry,
I sharpened pencils, played with clips,
Made feeble jokes and did not worry.

While at my desk I dawdled on
By lamp-light on an early morning,
The winter had appeared and gone-
A wasted and unheeded warning.

Autumn

I have allowed my family to scatter,
All those who were my dearest to depart,
And once again an age-long loneliness
Comes in to fill all nature and my heart.

Alone this cottage shelters me and you:
The wood is an unpeopled wilderness
And ways and footpaths wear, as in the song.
Weeds almost overgrowing each recess;

And where we sit together by ourselves
The log walls gaze upon us mournfully.
We gave no promise to leap obstacles,
We shall yet face our end with honesty.

At one we'll sit, at three again we'll rise,
My book with me, your sewing in your hand,
Nor with the dawning shall we realize
When all our kissing shall have had an end.

You leaves, more richly and more recklessly
Rustle your dresses, spill yourselves away,
And fill a past day's cup of bitterness
Still higher with the anguish of today!

All this delight, devotion and desire!
We'll fling ourselves into September's riot!
Immure yourself within the autumn's rustle
Entirely: go crazy, or be quiet!

How when you fall into my gentle arms
Enrobed in that silk-tasselled dressing gown
You shake the dress you wear away from you
As only coppices shake their leaves down!-

You are the blessing on my baneful way,
When life has depths worse than disease can reach,
And courage is the only root of beauty,
And it is this that draws us each to each.

Beloved, with the spent and sickly fumes...

Beloved, with the spent and sickly fumes
Of rumour's cinders all the air is filled,
But you are the engrossing lexicon
Of fame mysterious and unrevealed,

And fame it is the soil's strong pull.
Would that I more erect were sprung!
But even so I shall be called
The native son of my own native tongue.

The poets' age no longer sets their rhyme,
Now, in the sweep of country plots and roads,
Lermontov is rhymed with summertime,
And Pushkin rhymes with geese and snow.

And my wish is that when we die,
Our circle closed, and hence depart,
We shall be set in closer rhyme
Than binds the auricle and the heart.

And may our harmony unified
Some listener's muffled ear caress
With all that we do now imbibe,
And shall draw in through mouths of grass.

Confession

Life returned with a cause-the way
Some strange chance once interrupted it.
Just as on that distant summer day,
I am standing in the same old street.

People are the same, and people's worries,
And the sunset's still a fireball,
Just the way death's night once in a hurry
Nailed it to the ancient mansion's wall.

Women, in the same cheap clothes attired,
Are still wearing down their shoes at night.
Afterwards, against the roofing iron
They are by the garrets crucified.

Here is one of them. She looks so weary
As she steps across the threshold, and
Rising from the basement, drab and dreary,
Walks across the courtyard on a slant.

And again I'm ready with excuses,
And again it's all the same to me.
And the neighbour in the backyard pauses,
Then goes out of sight, and leaves us be.

———

Don't cry, do not purse your lips up,
They're puffy as it is, dear.
Mind you don't break the drying scab
Of smouldering spring fever.

Your hand is on my breast. Let go!
We are like two live wires.
If we aren't careful, we'll be thrown
Together unawares.

The years will pass, you'll marry yet
And you'll forget this squalor.

To be a woman is a feat,
To drive men mad, that's valour.

And as for me, I've been in thrall
For ages-begged like alms,
And worshipped the great miracle
Of woman's neck, back, arms.

Though bound tight, at the end of day,
By the anguished darkness' loop,
I'm ever lured to get away-
I long to break things up.

Definition of Poetry

It's a whistle blown ripe in a trice,
It's the cracking of ice in a gale,
It's a night that turns green leaves to ice,
It's a duel of two nightingales.

It is sweet-peas run gloriously wild,
It's the world's twinking tears in the pod,
It is Figaro like hot hail hurled
From the flutes on the wet flower bed.

It is all that the night hopes to find
On the bottom of deep bathing pools,
It's the star carried to the fish-pond
In your hands, wet and trembling and cool.

This close air is as flat as the boards
In the pond. The sky's flat on its face.
It would be fun if these stars guffawed-
But the universe is a dull place.

Fairy Tale

Once, in times forgotten,
In a fairy place,
Through the steppe, a rider
Made his way apace.

While he sped to battle,
Nearing from the dim
Distance, a dark forest
Rose ahead of him.

Something kept repeating,
Seemed his heart to graze:
Tighten up the saddle,
Fear the watering-place.

But he did not listen.
Heeding but his will,
At full speed he bounded
Up the wooded hill;

Rode into a valley,
Turning from the mound,
Galloped through a meadow,
Skirted higher ground;

Reached a gloomy hollow,
Found a trail to trace
Down the woodland pathway
To the watering-place.

Deaf to voice of warning,
And without remorse,
Down the slope, the rider
Led his thirsty horse.

———

Where the stream grew shallow,
Winding through the glen,

94

Eerie flames lit up the
Entrance to a den.

Through thick clouds of crimson
Smoke above the spring,
An uncanny calling
Made the forest ring.

And the rider started,
And with peering eye
Urged his horse in answer
To the haunting cry.

Then he saw the dragon,
And he gripped his lance;
And his horse stood breathless
Fearing to advance.

Thrice around a maiden
Was the serpent wound;
Fire-breathing nostrils
Cast a glare around.

And the dragon's body
Moved his scaly neck,
At her shoulder snaking
Whiplike forth and back.

By that country's custom
Was a young and fair
Captive brought as ransom
To the dragon's lair.

This then was the tribute
That the people owed
To the worm-protection
For a poor abode.

Now the dragon hugged his
Victim in alarm,
And the coils grew tighter
Round her throat and arm.

Skyward looked the horseman
With imploring glance,
And for the impending
Fight he couched his lance.

———

Tightly closing eyelids.
Heights and cloudy spheres.
Rivers. Waters. Boulders.
Centuries and years.

Helmetless, the wounded
Lies, his life at stake.
With his hooves the charger
Tramples down the snake.

On the sand, together-
Dragon, steed, and lance;
In a swoon the rider,
The maiden-in a trance.

Blue the sky; soft breezes
Tender noon caress.
Who is she? A lady?
Peasant girl? Princess?

Now in joyous wonder
Cannot cease to weep;
Now again abandoned
To unending sleep.

Now, his strength returning,
Opens up his eyes;
Now anew the wounded
Limp and listless lies.

But their hearts are beating.
Waves surge up, die down;
Carry them, and waken,
And in slumber drown.

96

Tightly closing eyelids.
Heights and cloudy spheres.
Rivers. Waters. Boulders.
Centuries and years.

Fiat

Heights and cloudy spheres.
Rivers. Wheres. Boulders.

Dawn will set candles guttering.
It will light up and loose the swifts.
With this reminder I'll burst in:
Let life be just as fresh as this!

Dawn's like a gunshot in the dark.
A bang-and flying burning bits
Of wadding go out, spark by spark.
Let life be just as fresh as this.

Another guest outside's the wind.
At night, it huddled close to us.
It's shivering-at dawn, it rained.
Let life be just as fresh as this.

It's so ridiculous and vain!
Why did it want to guard this place?
It saw the "No admittance" sign.
Let life be just as fresh as this.

I'll do your bidding at a sign-
A wave of kerchief-now,
While in the darkness you still reign
And while the fire's not out.

From early dawn the thirtieth of April...

Of ripened years will shoot up, piece the smell
Of humid centifolic. It will have to
Reveal itself, it cannot help but tell

From early dawn the thirtieth of April
Is given up to children of the town,
And caught in trying on the festive necklace,
By dusk it only just is settling down.

Like heaps of squashy berries under muslin
The town emerges out of crimson gauze.
Along the streets the boulevards are dragging
Their twilight with them, like a rank of dwarves.

The evening world is always eve and blossom,
But this one with a sprouting of its own
From May-day anniversaries will flower
One day into a commune fully blown.

For long it will remain a day of shifting,
Pre-festive cleaning, fanciful decor,
As once it used to be with Whitsun birches
Or pan-Athenian fires long before.

Just so they will go on, conveying actors
To their assembly points; beat sand; just so
Pull up towards illuminated ledges
The plywood boards, the crimson calico.

Just so in threes the sailors briskly walking
Will skirt the grass in gardens and in parks,
The moon at nightfall sink into the pavements
Like a dead city or a burnt-out hearth.

But with each year more splendid and more spreading
The taut beginning of the rose will bloom,
More clearly grow in health and sense of honour,
Sincerity more visibly will loom.

The living folksongs, customs and traditions
Will ever spreading, many-petalled lay
Their scent on fields and industries and meadows
From early buddings on the first of May,

Until the full fermented risen spirit
Of ripened years will shoot up, like the smell
Of humid centifolia. It will have to
Reveal itself, it cannot help but tell.

Here a riddle has drawn a strange nailmark

Here a riddle has drawn a strange nailmark. To sleep now!
I'll reread, understand with the light of the sun,
But until I am wakened, to touch the beloved
As I do has been given to none.

How I touched you! So touched were you even by the copper
Of my lips, as an audience is touched by a play,
And the kiss was like summer; it lingered and lingered,
Only later the thunderstorm came.

And I drank in long draughts, like the birds, half-unconscious.
The stars trickle slowly through the throat to the crop,
While the nightingales roll up their eyes in a shudder
From the firmament draining the night drop by drop.

Hops

Beneath the willow wound round with ivy
we take cover from the worst
of the storm, with a greatcoat round
our shoulders and my hands around your waist.

I've got it wrong. That isn't ivy
entwined in the bushes round
the wood, but hops. You intoxicate me!
Let's spread the greatcoat on the ground.

I grew. Foul weather, dreams, forebodings...

I grew. Foul weather, dreams, forebodings
    Were bearing me - a Ganymede -
Away from earth; distress was growing
    Like wings - to spread, to hold, to lead.

I grew. The veil of woven sunsets
    At dusk would cling to me and swell.
With wine in glasses we would gather
    To celebrate a sad farewell,

And yet the eagle's clasp already
    Refreshes forearms' heated strain.
The days have gone, when, love, you floated
    Above me, harbinger of pain.

Do we not share the sky, the flying?
    Now, like a swan, his death-song done,
Rejoice! In triumph, with the eagle
    Shoulder to shoulder, we are one.

Imitators

A boat came in; the cliff was baked;
The noisy boat-chain fell and clanked on
    The sand-an iron rattle-snake,
A rattling rust among the plankton.

And two got out; and from the cliff
I felt like calling down, 'Forgive me,
But would you kindly throw yourselves
    Apart or else into the river?

Your miming is without a fault-
Of course the seeker finds the fancied-
But stop this playing with the boat!
Your model on the cliff resents it.'

In Hospital

They stood, almost blocking the pavement,
As though at a window display;
The stretcher was pushed in position,
The ambulance started away.

Past porches and pavements and people
It plunged with its powerful light
Through streets in nocturnal confusion
Deep into the blackness of night.

The headlights picked out single faces,
Militiamen, stretches of street.
The nurse with a smelling-salts phial
Was rocked to and fro on her seat.

A drain gurgled drearily. Cold rain
Was falling. The hospital-clerk
Took out a fresh form of admission
And filled it in, mark upon mark.

They gave him a bed by the entrance;
No room in the ward could be found.
Strong iodine vapour pervaded
The draught from the windows around.

His window framed part of the garden,
And with it a bit of the sky.
The newcomer studied the floorboards,
The ward and the objects nearby,

When, watching the nurse's expression
Of doubt, in her questioning drive,
He suddenly knew this adventure
Would hardly release him alive.

Then, grateful, he turned to the window
Behind which the wall, further down,
Was breathing like smouldering tinder,
Lit up by the glare of the town.

There, far off the city was glowing
All crimson-aflame; in its swell
A maple-branch, ragged, was bowing
To bid him a silent farewell.

'o Lord,' he was thinking, 'how perfect
Thy works are, how perfect and right;
The walls and the beds and the people,
This death-night, the city at night!

'I drink up a sedative potion,
And weeping, my handkerchief trace.
o Father, the tears of emotion
Prevent me from seeing Thy face.

'Dim light scarcely touches my bedstead.
It gives me such comfort to drift
And feel that my life and my lot are
Thy priceless and wonderful gift.

'While dying in fading surroundings
I feel how Thy hands are ablaze,
The hands that have made me and hold me
And hide like a ring in a case.'

It is not seemly to be famous...

It is not seemly to be famous:
Celebrity does not exalt;
There is no need to hoard your writings
And to preserve them in a vault.

To give your all-this is creation,
And not-to deafen and eclipse.
How shameful, when you have no meaning,
To be on everybody's lips!

Try not to live as a pretender,
But so to manage your affairs
That you are loved by wide expanses,
And hear the call of future years.

Leave blanks in life, not in your papers,
And do not ever hesitate
To pencil out whole chunks, whole chapters
Of your existence, of your fate.

Into obscurity retiring
Try your development to hide,
As autumn mist on early mornings
Conceals the dreaming countryside.

Another, step by step, will follow
The living imprint of your feet;
But you yourself must not distinguish
Your victory from your defeat.

And never for a single moment
Betray your credo or pretend,
But be alive-this only matters-
Alive and burning to the end.

Lessons of English

When Desdemona sang a ditty-
In her last hours among the living-
It wasn't love that she lamented,
And not her star-she mourned a willow.
When Desdemona started singing,
With tears near choking off her voice,
Her evil demon for her evil day
Stored up of weeping rills a choice.

And when Ophelia sang a ballad-
In her last hours among the living-
All dryness of her soul was carried
Aloft by gusts of wind, like cinders.

The day Ophelia started singing,
By bitterness of daydreams jaded,
What trophies did she clutch, when sinking?
A bunch of buttercups and daisies.

Their shoulders stripped of passion's tatters,
They took, their hearts a-quake with fear,
The Universe's chilly baptism-
To stun their loving forms with spheres.

Margarita

Sundering the bushes like a snare,
More violet than Margarita's tight-pressed lips,
More passionate than Margarita's white-eyed stare,
The nightingale glowed, royally throbbed and trilled.

Like the scent of grass ascending,
Like the crazed rainfall's mercury, the foliage among,
He stupefied the bark, approached the mouth, panting,
And, halting there, upon a braid he hung.

When Margarita to the light was drawn,
Stroking her eyes with an astonished hand,
It seemed, beneath the helm of branch and rain,
A weary Amazon was fallen to the ground.

Her head in her hand in his hand lay,
Her other arm was bent back up to where,
Dangling, there hung her helmet of shade,
Sundering the branches like a snare.

109

Meeting

The snow will dust the roadway,
And load the roofs still more.
I'll stretch my legs a little:
You're there outside the door.

Autumn, not winter coat,
Hat-none, galoshes-none.
You struggle with excitement
Out there all on your own.

Far, far into the darkness
Fences and trees withdraw.
You stand there on the corner,
Under the falling snow.

The water trickles down from
The kerchief that you wear
Into your sleeves, while dewdrops
Shine sparkling in your hair.

And now illumined by
A single strand of light
Are features, kerchief, figure
And coat of autumn cut.

There's wet snow on your lashes
And in your eyes, distress,
And your external image
Is all, all of apiece.

As if an iron point
With truly consummate art,
Dipped into antimony,
Had scribed you on my heart.

Those modest, humble features
Are in it now to stay,
And if the world's cruel-hearted,
That's merely by the way.

And therefore it is doubled,
All this night in snow;
To draw frontiers between us
Is more than I can do.

But who are we and whence,
If, of those years gone by,
Scandal alone remains
And we have ceased to be.

Night

The night proceeds and dwindling
Prepares the day's rebirth.
An airman is ascending
Above the sleeping earth.

And almost disappearing
In cloud, a tiny spark,
He now is like a cross-stitch,
A midget laundry-mark.

Beneath him are strange cities,
And heavy traffic-lanes,
And night-clubs, barracks, stokers,
And railways, stations, trains.

The shadow of his wing-span
Falls heavy on the cloud.
Celestial bodies wander
Around him in a crowd.

And there, with frightful listing
Through emptiness, away
Through unknown solar systems
Revolves the Milky Way.

In limitless expanses
Are headlands burning bright.
In basements and in cellars
The stokers work all night.

And underneath a rooftop
In Paris, maybe Mars
Or Venus sees a notice
About a recent farce.

And maybe in an attic
And under ancient slates
A man sits wakeful, working,
He thinks and broods and waits;

He looks upon the planet,
As if the heavenly spheres
Were part of his entrusted
Nocturnal private cares.

Fight off your sleep: be wakeful,
Work on, keep up your pace,
Keep vigil like the pilot,
Like all the stars in space.

Work on, work on, creator-
To sleep would be a crime-
Eternity's own hostage,
And prisoner of Time.

Oh terrible, beloved! A poet's loving

Oh terrible, beloved! A poet's loving
Is a restless god's passionate rage,
And chaos out into the world comes creeping,
As in the ancient fossil age.

His eyes weep him mist by the ton,
Enveloped in tears he is mammoth-like,
Out of fashion. He knows it must not be done.
Ages have passed-he does not know why.

He sees wedding parties all around,
Drunken unions celebrated unaware,
Common frogspawn found in every pond
Ritually adorned as precious caviare.

Like some Watteau pearl, how cleverly
A snuffbox embraces all life's matter,
And vengeance is wreaked on him, probably
Because, where they distort and flatter,

Where simpering comfort lies and fawns,
Where they rub idle shoulders, crawl like drones,
He will raise your sister from the ground,
Use her like a bacchante from the Grecian urns,

And pour into his kiss the Andes' melting,
And morning in the steppe, under the sway
Of dusted stars, as night's pallid bleating
Bustles about the village on its way.

And the botanical vestry's dense blackness,
And all the ravine's age-old breath,
Waft over the ennui of the stuffed mattress,
And the forest's ancient chaos spurts forth

On The Steamer

The stir of leaves, the chilly morning air
Were like delirium; half awake
Jaws clamped; the dawn beyond the Kama glared
Blue, as the plumage of a drake.

There was a clattering of crockery,
A yawning steward taking stock,
And in the depth, as high as candlesticks,
Within the river, glow-worms flocked.

They hung from streets along the waterfront,
A scintillating string; it chimed
Three times; the steward with a napkin tried
To scratch away some candle grime.

Like a grey rumour, crawling from the past,
A mighty epic of the reeds,
With ripples in the beads of street lamps, fast
Towards Perm the Kama ran upon a breeze.

Choking on waves, and almost drowning, but
Still swimming on beyond the boat
A star kept diving and resurfacing
An icon's shining light afloat.

A smell of paint mixed with the galley smells,
And on the Kama all along,
The twilight drifted, secrets gathering,
With not a splash it drifted on...

A glass in hand, your pupils narrowing
You watched the slips of tongue perform
A whirling play on words, at suppertime,
But were not drawn into their swarm.

You called your partner to old happenings,
To waves of days before your day,
To plunge in them, a final residue
Of the last drop, and fade away.

The stir of leaves in chilly morning air
Was like delirium; half awake
One yawned; the east beyond the Kama glared
Blue, as the plumage of a drake.

And, like a bloodbath now the morning came,
A flaming flood of oil - to drown
The steamer's gaslights in the stateroom and
The waning street lamps of the town.

Ploughing Time

What is the matter with the landscape?
Familiar landmarks are not there.
Ploughed fields, like squares upon a chessboard,
Today are scattered everywhere.

The newly-harrowed vast expanses
So evenly are spread about,
As though the valley had been spring-cleaned
Or else the mountains flattened out.

And that same day, in one endeavour,
Outside the furrows every tree
Bursts into leaf, light-green and downy,
And stretches skyward, tall and free.

No speck of dust on the new maples,
And colours nowhere are as clean
As is the light-grey of the ploughland
And as the silver-birch's green.

So they begin. With two years gone...

So they begin. With two years gone
From nurse to countless tunes they scuttle.
They chirp and whistle. Then comes on
The third year, and they start to prattle.

So they begin to see and know.
In din of started turbines roaring
Mother seems not their mother now,
And you not you, and home is foreign.

What meaning has the menacing
Beauty beneath the lilac seated,
If to steal children's not the thing?
So first they fear that they are cheated.

So ripen fears. Can he endure
A star to beat him in successes,
When he's a Faust, a sorcerer?
So first his gipsy life progresses.

So from the fence where home should lie
In flight above are found to hover
Seas unexpected as a sigh.
So first iambics they discover.

So summer nights fall down and pray
"Thy will be done" where oats are sprouting,
And menace with your eyes the day.
So with the sun they start disputing.

So verses start them on their way.

Sparrow Hills

My kisses across your breast, like water from a jug!
They'll have an end, and soon, our days of summer heat.
Nor shall we every night rise up in trailing dust
The hurdy-gurdy's bellow, stamp and drag our feet.

I've heard about old age. What ominous forebodings!
That no wave will lift again to the stars its hands,
That waters will speak no more; no god in the woods;
No heart within the pools; no life in meadowlands.

O rouse your soul! This frenzied day is yours to have!
It is the world's midday. Why don't you use your eyes?
Look, there's thought upon high hills in seething bubbles
Of heat, woodpeckers, cones and needles, clouds and skies.

Here tracks of city trolleys stop, and further
The pines alone must satisfy. Trams cannot pass.
It is always Sunday there! Plucking little branches,
There the clearing capers, slipping on the grass.

And strewing sunrays, Whitsun, and rambling walks,
The woods will have us say the world was always so:
Conceived like that by forests, hinted to the meadows,
And spilt by clouds as on a chintz design below.

Spring Shower

Winked to the birdcherry, gulped amid tears,
Splashed over carriages' varnish, trees' tremble.
Full moon. The musicians are picking their way
To the theatre. More and more people assemble.

Puddles on stone. Like a throat overfilled
With tears are the roses, deep with wet scalding
Diamonds. Showers of gladness thrill,
Eyelashes, stormclouds, and roses enfolding.

The moon for the first time is casting in plaster
An epic poem uncast till today:
The cordons, the flutter of dresses, the speaker
And people enraptured and carried away.

Whose is the heart whose whole blood shot to glory
Drained from the cheeks? We are held in his grip.
The hands of Kerensky are squeezing together
Into a bunch our aortas and lips.

This is not night, not rain, not a chorus
Of tearing acclaim for him, swelled to a roar-
This is the blinding leap to the Forum
From catacombs wanting an exit before.

It is not roses, not Ups, not the roaring
Crowd-it's the surf on Theatre Square,
Marking the end of the long sleep of Europe,
Proud of her own reawakening here.

The garden scatters burnt-up beetles...

The garden scatters burnt-up beetles
Like brazen ash, from braziers burst.
I witness, by my lighted candle,
A newly blossomed universe.

And like a not yet known religion
I enter this unheard of night,
In which the shabbily-grey poplar
Has curtained off the lunar light.

The pond is a presented secret.
Oh, whispers of the appletree!
The garden hangs-a pile construction,
And holds the sky in front of me.

The patient watches

The patient watches. Six days long
In frenzy blizzards rave relentlessly,
Roll over rooftops, roar along,
Brace, rage, and fall, collapsing senselessly.

In snowstorms Christmas is consumed.
He dreams: they came and lifted someone.
He starts: "Whom? Me?" There was a call,
A tolling bell... Not New Year's summons?

Far, in the Kremlin, booms Ivan,
Dives, drowns, resounds in swaying motion.
He sleeps. When great, a blizzard can
Be called Pacific, as the Ocean.

The shiv'ring piano, foaming at the mouth

The shiv'ring piano, foaming at the mouth,
Will wrench you by its ravings, discompose you.
"My darling," you will murmur. "No!" I'll shout.
"To music?!" Yet can two be ever closer

Than in the dusk, while tossing vibrant chords
Into the fireplace, like journals, tome by tome?
Oh, understanding wonderful, just nod,
And you will know I do not claim to own

Your soul and body. You may go where'er
You want. To others. Werther has been written
Already. Death these days is in the air.
One opens up one's veins much like a window.

The Weeping Garden

The garden is frightful! It drips, it listens:
Is it in loneliness here,
Crushing a branch like lace at a window,
Or is there a witness near?

The earth is heavy with swollen burdens;
Smothered, the spongy weald.
Listen! Afar, as though it were August,
Night ripens in a field.

No sound. Not a stranger around to spy.
Feeling deserted, alone,
It starts up again, dripping and tumbling
On roof, gutter, flagstone.

I'll bring it close to my lips, and listen:
Am I in loneliness here,
Ready to burst with tears in darkness,
Or is there a witness near?

Deep silence. Not even a leaf is astir.
No gleam of light to be seen.
Only choking sobs and the splash of slippers
And sighs and tears between.

Things of great worth shall come to pass...

Things of great worth shall come to pass
By true foreknowledge and in fact,—
Names worthier than mine in fame
And words which earned me men's esteem.

Here breakers roar across the bay;
Wave follows wave unchangeably,
Their tracks, like letters traced in sand,
Erased by ebbing lines of foam.

So yet you're here at this resort.
I should have found you in this hall
At five, instead of vain small talk
I shared and wagging of my tongue.

I would have warned you, one so fair,
Mature, a woman brave and calm,
About the death in life-and bounds
No higher than the ant's low life.

Great poets, through experience,
Find words so simple and restrained
That in the end they can't do more
Than wait in silence and in awe.

In faith and kinship with real life
And with the future knit as one,
We're bound to find immortal words
Of unbelievable simplicity.

Yet keep them holy in your hearts
Or we shall not be spared at all.
Men quickly grasp the complex schemes
When simplicity's their greater need.

To Anna Akhmatova

It seems I'm choosing the essential words
That I can liken to your pristine power.
And if I err, it's all the same to me,
For I shall cling to all my errors still.

I hear the constant patter on wet roofs,
The smothered eclogue of the wooden pavements.
A certain city comes clear in every line,
And springs to life in every syllable.

The roads are blocked, despite the tide of spring
All round. Your clients are a stingy, cruel lot.
Bent over piles of work, the sunset burns;
Eyes blear and moist from sewing by a lamp.

You long for the boundless space of Ladoga,
And hasten, weary, to the lake for change
And rest. It's little in the end you gain.
The canals smell rank like musty closet-chests.

And like an empty nut the hot wind frets
Across their waves, across the blinking eyelids
Of stars and branches, posts and lamps, and one
Lone seamstress gazing far above the bridge.

I know that eyes and objects vary greatly
In singleness and sharpness, yet the essence
Of greatest strength, dissolving fear, is the sky
At night beneath the gaze of polar light.

That's how I call to mind your face and glance.
No, not the image of that pillar of salt
Exalts me now, in which five years ago
You set in rhymes our fear of looking back.

But as it springs in all your early work,
Where crumbs of unremitting prose grew strong,
In all affairs, like wires conducting sparks,
Your work throbs high with our remembered past.

Try and don't let me grieve

Try and don't let me grieve. Come and try to extinguish
This wild onslaught of sadness that rumbles like mercury in
Torricellian void.
Madness, try and forbid me to feel, come and try!
Do not let me rant on about you! We're alone-don't be shy.
Now, extinguish it, do! Only-hotter!

Wet Paint

'Look out! Wet paint.' My soul was blind,
    I have to pay the price,
All marked with stains of calves and cheeks
    And hands and lips and eyes.

I loved you more than luck or grief
    Because with you in sight
The old and yellowed world became
    As white as painters' white.

I swear my friend, my gloom-it will
    One day still whiter gleam,
Than lampshades, than a bandaged brow,
    Than a delirious dream.

Wind

I am no more but you live on,
And the wind, whining and complaining,
Is shaking house and forest, straining
Not single fir trees one by one
But the whole wood, all trees together,
With all the distance far and wide,
Like sail-less yachts in stormy weather
When moored within a bay they lie.
And this not out of wanton pride
Or fury bent on aimless wronging,
But to provide a lullaby
For you with words of grief and longing,

Without A Title

So aloof, so meek in your ways,
Now you're fire, you're pure combustion.
Only let me lock up your beauty
Deep, deep down in a poem's dungeon.

See how wholly transformed they are
By the fire in the glowing lampshade;
Edge of wall, edge of window-pane,
Our own figures and our own shadows.

There you sit on cushions, apart,
Legs tucked under you, Turkish fashion.
In the light or in the shadow,
Childlike, always, the way you reason.

Dreaming, now you thread on a string
Beads that lie on your lap in profusion.
Far too sad is your mien, too artless
Is the drift of your conversation.

Yes, love's truly a vulgar word.
I'll invent something else to supplant it,
Just for you, the whole world, all words
I will gladly rename, if you want it.

Can your sorrowful mien convey
All your hidden orebearing richness,
All that radiant seam of your heart?
Why d'you fill your eyes with such sadness?

CPSIA information can be obtained
at www.ICGtesting.com
Printed in the USA
BVHW040156200123
656710BV00014B/113/J

9 781636 379968